Brian Patten

Mouse Poems

Michelle Cartlidge

SCHOLASTIC
PRESS

MORNING

Time to wake, sleepy-heads,

So come on, up with you!

The bluebells are chiming,

The harebells too.

Primroses are bathing

In the morning dew.

READING

The headlines in The Daily Mouse

Are all quite wonderful today:

Mice Have Landed On The Moon!

The Ginger Tom Is Going Away!

THE POST MOUSE

Letters from Africa, postcards from Peru,

Parcels from Jamaica and from London, too!

Orange stamps and green stamps,

Red stamps and bright blue,

The post mouse is bringing

All this mail for you.

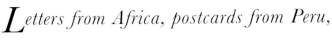

IN THE GARDEN

Out on the garden wall
  The fat old cat is sleeping,
Underneath the roses
  The garden mice are creeping,
While down from the tree-tops
  Twenty-one birds are peeping.

The Rocking Horse

Clippity-clippity-clippity clop,

Riding a rocking horse in a toy shop.

Clippity-clippity-clippity clop,

Cling on tight or off you will drop!

THE BUSKER

Sad songs and glad songs,

Quiet songs and loud,

The mouse sings his heart out

For the passing crowd.

DRESSING UP

"*Mirror, mirror, on the wall,*

Who's the best dressed mouse of all?"

"Is it me?"

"Or me?"

"Or me?"

"Or me?"

"Or me?"

"Or me?"

The Play

Mice in the theatre, putting on a play

All about the pirates down in Pirate Bay.

The play will be over just in time for tea.

They'll have it sitting on the stage

Beside the painted sea.

THE ACROBATS

Balancing on the tightrope,

Swinging on the trapeze,

The fabulous acrobatic mice

Perform their tricks with ease.

THE WITCH

Witchery witchery witchery woo,

Old mouse-witch, how do you do?

Up on your broomstick in the night sky,

How do you make that old broom fly?

BATHTIME

"*You're a grubby lot,*" *scolds Mother Mouse.*

"*Goodness knows where you have been.*

You'd better let me wash you now . . .

Or the cat might lick you clean!"

BEDTIME

Sleepyheads, it's bedtime,

It is time to go to sleep.

Mummy will look in later

To make sure your sleep is deep.